8-10

The purchase of this item was
made possible by Collection
Development money award by
the 2007 Nevada Legislature.

THE ESSENTIAL GUIDE

Brian Bromberg

Contents:

Go, Diego, Go!   4

Diego   6

Animal Rescue Center   8

Baby Jaguar   10

Rescue Pack   12

Click   14

Rescue tools   16

Bobo Brothers   18

Sammy the Sloth   20

Linda the Llama   22

Tuga the Turtle   24

¡La familia!   26

Dinosaur rescue!   28

Rain forest floor   30

Rain forest canopy   32

Rain forest river   34

Cloud Forest 36

Mountain 38

Ocean 40

Antarctica 42

Desert 44

Grasslands 45

Africa 46

Go, Diego, Go!

¡Al rescate! To the rescue with Diego! This rough-and-tumble Animal Rescuer is always ready to leap into action to save the animals of the rain forest—and beyond! Baby Jaguar, his sister Alicia, and more will lend a hand, but Diego also needs your help on his heroic missions. Help him to update his field journal by answering the questions. Find all the answers on p48!

Diego

Diego Marquez is an Animal Rescuer who will do anything to help animals in trouble. Whether he's assisting at the Animal Rescue Center or racing through the rain forest, there's no rescue too big and no animal too small for Diego!

Animal scientist

Diego uses his computer, Field Journal, and more to learn all he can about animals. But this scientist doesn't spend much time in the lab! Diego is in-the-know AND on-the-go!

Animal Rescuers wear a Rescue Patch.

Baby Jaguar

Diego can always count on his furry friend Baby Jaguar to help him on his rescue missions.

Diego's Video Watch allows him to communicate with other Animal Rescuers.

To the rescue!

Diego doesn't save all those animals alone! He gets help from Baby Jaguar, his sister Alicia, Rescue Pack, Click the Camera, and YOU!

Rescue Pack has got Diego's back! He can turn into anything Diego needs!

Diego's Mami cares for a baby caiman at the Animal Rescue Center.

What a team!

Diego and Baby Jaguar are close friends and go on most rescue missions together.

Like mother, like son!

Diego's entire family helps animals at their Animal Rescue Center, deep in the rain forest.

Did You Know?

- Diego wears his Video Watch on his left wrist.
- Diego can drive.
- Diego speaks English and Spanish.

Animal Rescue Center

Diego and his family run the Animal Rescue Center, a science outpost in the rain forest where animals in trouble can find help, and, of course, great friends too!

The Rescue Computer has lots of information about animals.

The Science Deck

From the Science Deck Diego can ride a zip cord down to the forest floor to find animals in trouble!

Diego can:

- Use Click the Camera to find animals in trouble

- Help lost or hurt animals

- Get info from the Rescue Computer

Cool tools!

Diego has lots of great rescue tools that he keeps at the Animal Rescue Center, like his trusty Spotting Scope

The Animal Rescue Center overlooks the rain forest.

Computer wiz!
Alicia can find useful animal information on the Rescue Computer to aid Diego.

How many science tools do you see in the Animal Rescue Center?

The Animal Rescuers use this First Aid pack to help injured animals.

Animal Photo Album
Whenever Diego helps an animal, he prints its picture from the computer, and then stores it in the Animal Photo Album.

9

Baby Jaguar

This playful young jaguar is Diego's best friend in the rain forest. He loves using his jaguar skills to join Diego on his rescue missions.

Get the point?
Like all jaguars, Baby Jaguar has sharp claws for climbing!

Animal & rescuer!

Baby Jaguar hopes to earn his Rescue Patch like Diego. He wants to be an Animal Rescuer too!

A jaguar can wave its tail over water to go "fishing!"

Hide-and-seek!
Jaguars are great hiders because their spots help them blend into the colorful rain forest.

Mreow, Mreow!

Baby Jaguar swings into action with Diego!

Jaguar power!
What can Baby Jaguar do? Let's review!

 Run! ¡Corre!

 Jump! ¡Salta!

 Climb! ¡Sube!

Rescue Pack

Rescue Pack has got your back! That's because he's a messenger bag that can turn into anything to help Diego on his rescue missions. Just say, "*¡Actívate!*" to make him spring into action!

Rescue Pack doesn't carry much because he can transform into whatever Diego needs!

Slide to the rescue!

Rescue Pack can turn into a mud board to help Diego surf down a slippery mountain.

Rescue Pack's board has also helped Diego surf on water and snow.

High-flyer!

When Diego needs to reach the top of a tall mountain, Rescue Pack can turn into a hot-air balloon to get him there.

Soar into the sky with Rescue Pack!

Wild water scooter!

Diego can ask Rescue Pack to turn into a water scooter to zip through the waves.

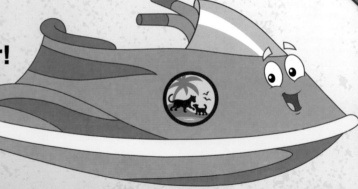

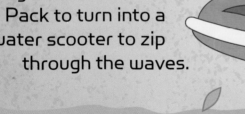

¡Actívate!

River rescue!
Diego and Baby Jaguar always remember to stay safe with life jackets and helmets!

Field Journal Update!
To get over a deep gorge, what should Rescue Pack turn into?

A parasail?

A raft?

A kayak?

Click

Part telescopic camera and part animal locator, Click is Diego's "flashy" friend at the Animal Rescue Center who can zoom through the rain forest to find the animal in need of Diego's help.

Sound waves travel through Click's lens when an animal cries for help.

How many legs does Click have? *¡Cuatro!* Four!

Click comes, too!
Sometimes Click goes with Diego to take pictures for the Animal Photo Album.

Animal finder
Most of Diego's rescue missions begin with Click finding the animal in trouble and showing it to him.

Puma problems
Click finds a puma who needs to get home to the mountains.

Look in the lens
Click shows Diego the animals that he needs to help.

Say, "Click! Take a pic!"

Penguin pic
In icy Antarctica, Diego needs Click's help to find a baby penguin!

How many animals has Click found on these two pages?

Actual Animal Photos!
Alicia can also use the Rescue Computer to find animal photos. What animal does she have here?

 It has dark spots.

 It can climb trees.

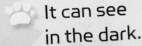 It can see in the dark.

 It's a big cat.

Alicia puts it in the Animal Photo Album!

It's a jaguar!

15

Rescue tools

Rescue Pack can turn into a tent for Diego's overnight rescues!

Gadgets, gizmos, and vehicles galore help Diego go, go, go to any animal! Some tools, like his Video Watch, keep him in contact with the Animal Rescue Center while others, like the Rescue Truck, get him further into the field!

Field Journal

Diego can find any fact about animals, plants, and environments in his Field Journal, a portable computerized data bank of useful information!

Here are some other tools that have come in handy on Diego's missions:

 Animal Snack Pack

 Rescue Flashlight

 Scuba Gear

Rescue Tow Cable and Hook.

To bring the tapir back home, Diego used:

Diego also used his binoculars to see the road to tell Chucho the Train where to go!

His Field Journal to find out where tapirs live.

His Spotting Scope to see in the distance.

His Video Watch to get more information from Alicia.

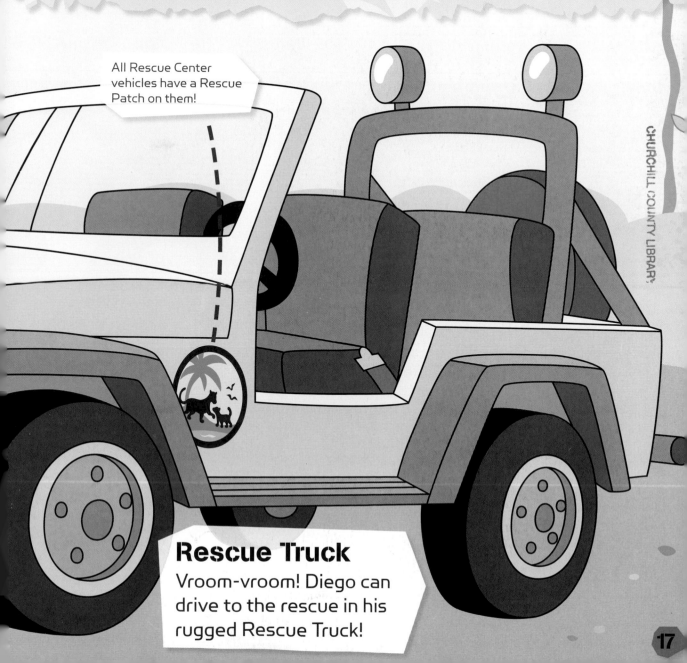

All Rescue Center vehicles have a Rescue Patch on them!

Rescue Truck

Vroom-vroom! Diego can drive to the rescue in his rugged Rescue Truck!

Bobo Brothers

These wild, mischievous spider monkeys are always causing trouble for Diego. They don't mean to make problems. They just get a little carried away when they're playing. To help Diego put a stop to the Bobo Brothers' mayhem, you need to say...

"FREEZE, BOBOS!"

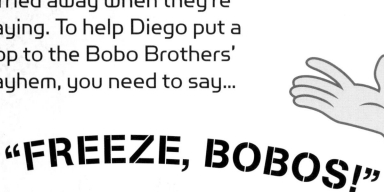

Bobos, Bobos!
When these silly monkeys are nearby, Diego can hear their silly call, "Bobos, Bobos!"

Monkeying around
The Bobo Brothers love to have a good time, although their playful ways make a mess for Diego!

18

They can always be seen together.

Oops! Sorry!

When Diego tells the Bobo Brothers to "freeze," they do—sometimes in mid-air! When they realize they're doing something wrong, they always say, "Oops! Sorry!"

Save the Bobos!
The Bobo Brothers need Diego's help when they get themselves into trouble!

Helpful Bobos

The Bobo Brothers don't always cause mischief. Sometimes, they help, like when they:

- Cleaned banana peels off the rainforest floor.
- Helped plant strawberries for the Strawberry Festival.
- Tried to help Diego stop a mean magician in the mountains!

The Bobo Brothers love to make music—especially on noisy instruments!

A careful climber!

Sloths like Sammy use their arms and legs to climb VERY slowly through the tree branches.

Diego moves like Sammy does!

Sammy the Sloth

Sammy the Sloth is Diego's rain forest friend who's always hanging out (upside-down from a tree) near the Animal Rescue Center. He's a slow-moving fellow, but that doesn't stop him from helping when he can!

Field Journal Update!

Which is a true fact about sloths?

🐾 Sloths live in big cities.

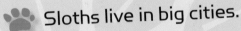

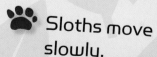 Sloths move slowly.

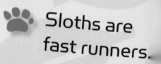 Sloths are fast runners.

Sharp claws for grabbing and holding tree branches!

A rare visit!
Sammy comes down to the ground to see Diego.

¡Uno, dos, tres!
Sammy is a three-toed sloth. And what sharp toes they are!

A true tree house!
Sloths live high up in the trees, close to their food!

Strong swimmers!
Sloths may be slow on land, but they're great swimmers!

Linda the Llama

¡Hola, Linda! Linda is a Spanish-speaking llama who lives high in the mountains. With her strong back and powerful legs, she can help Diego on all his mountain missions!

Llamas are great climbers. The pads on their feet stop them from slipping.

Yummy salad
Llamas like to graze on grass and hay.

Linda saves *Carnaval*!
When music and party goodies are needed at the *Carnaval*, Linda brings them up the mountain.

Linda to the Rescue!

Linda has helped Diego on some pretty important missions. She...

 Carried books up the mountain.

 Pulled a giant rock off a mountain path.

 Pulled Santa's sleigh out of the snow.

22

Long necks help llamas keep a look out for danger.

Strong and speedy

Linda is so strong and quick that she can run with Diego on her back!

Llamas have two toes on each foot.

Leader of the pack!

Llamas are pack animals. They can help people by carrying lots of stuff on their backs.

Tuga the Turtle

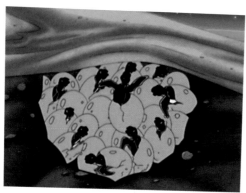

Tuga is Diego's Spanish-speaking friend of the sea. She's known his family for a long time and she's always happy to help on ocean rescues. Diego can even hitch a ride on this super swimmer's shell!

The Leatherback sea turtle is the largest sea turtle in the world!

Leatherback sea turtles can lay 150 eggs at a time! How many can you count here?

Egg-cellent!
The first thing newborn sea turtles do when they're born is dig themselves out of the sand!

Moving in moonlight
Newborn sea turtles follow the light of the moon to find their way back to sea.

Sea turtles can swim really fast through warm or cold waters!

Jelly, anyone?
Leatherback sea turtles don't have teeth, so they eat soft foods like jellyfish!

Turtle shell
A leatherback sea turtle's shell isn't hard. It feels soft and rubbery!

Leatherback sea turtles have strong flippers to swim through the sea.

¡La familia!

Diego comes from an entire family of Animal Rescuers. Joining him each day at the Animal Rescue Center are his *Mami*, his *Papi*, and his sister, Alicia. And don't forget his cousin Dora, who sometimes drops by for an adventure

Alicia has a Rescue Rope to swing to the rescue.

Alicia

Diego's 11-year-old sister loves helping animals just as much as he does. Many times, she joins Diego's rescue missions out in the field.

Download complete!

Saving animals together
Sometimes, the whole family goes on missions together.

Helpful sister
Alicia can find any animal information Diego needs for a rescue mission on the computer.

Everyone in Diego's family wears a Rescue Patch!

Count the people in Diego's family. Don't forget Dora!

Señor y Señora Marquez
Diego and Alicia learned their love and respect for animals from their parents, who run the Rescue Center.

27

Dinosaur rescue!

It's Diego's BIGGEST rescue yet when he jumps back in time with Baby Jaguar, Alicia, and even Dora to bring a mighty Maiasaura back to her dinosaur family!

Really old babies

Dinosaurs—like these baby Maiasauras—hatched from eggs, just like birds.

Euoplocephalus

One tough dinosaur! The euoplocephalus had built-in armor and a club-like tail for protection from bigger dinosaurs!

Spikes all over for extra defense!

Tyrannosaurus Rex

The terrifying T-Rex may have had two short front arms, but it also had huge legs for running, powerful jaws, and teeth almost as long as your arm!

Pterodactyl

Pterodactyls had wings between their fingers to help them soar through the prehistoric sky!

Strong claws for perching high on mountains!

Sharp claws on its feet for tearing!

Einiosaurus

Charge into adventure! The einiosaurus was a plant-eater, but it could protect itself from meat-eaters with its horns and armor-plates!

Strong legs for running like a rhino!

29

Rain forest floor

Bottom floor! There are plenty of animals large and small to rescue down here on the rain forest floor—from big animals like jaguars to animals as tiny as insects! Will you help Diego leap into action?

It stays really shady on the rain forest floor because of all the thick plants and trees covering it.

How many mammals do you see on the rain forest floor? Don't forget Diego!

Powerful eyes for seeing in the dark!

Strong legs for jumping really high!

Jaguar
These big cats have sharp claws for climbing and powerful legs for running fast.

Three-banded armadillo

This armored amigo is the only armadillo that can roll itself into a ball to protect itself with its hard shell.

Armadillos have short legs, but they can move quickly if they need to!

Sharp claws for digging burrows in the ground.

Red-eyed tree frog

Red-eyed tree frogs leave the water to live the "high life" in trees. They jump really high with powerful back legs!

Sticky, suction-cup-like toes for tree climbing!

Strong beaks for breaking open nuts and hard food!

Rainbow-colored wings carry them up into the trees.

Rain forest canopy

Look up! The rain forest canop has so many leaves and branches that it shades the whole forest! More animals the rain forest live here tha anywhere else—monkeys, snakes, birds, and mor Here are just a fev Diego has met

Scarlet macaw

This colorful bird lives in the treetops of the rain forest and eats bananas!

Climb time!
Scarlet macaws use their beaks to help them climb!

Kinkajoo

This treetop creature is related to a raccoon and is nocturnal—it sleeps during the day and is active at night.

Blue morpho butterfly

This master of disguise has bright blue wings on one side, but underneath, they're the same color as the tree leaves. When it folds its wings, it seems to disappear!

A caterpillar builds a chrysalis and emerges as a beautiful butterfly.

Short wings to zoom in and out of trees easily.

Harpy eagle

The harpy eagle is one of the biggest eagles in the world! It has strong talons for grabbing food and perching.

Rain forest river

Grab a raft and help Diego save the amazing animals in the rivers of the rain forest. Fish, reptiles, amphibians, and mammals all call freshwater rivers their home.

How many reptiles do you see? How many mammals?

River dolphin
Baby river dolphins are gray but turn pink when they grow up!

Strong tail to help it swim through the water.

Caiman
Caimans are cousins of alligators and crocodiles. They swim in fresh, still water.

River otter

River otters have long, sleek bodies that help them to zip and glide quickly through the water.

River otters can hold their breath for a long time and can see very well underwater.

Webbed feet for super-swimming!

Anacondas use their bodies to wrap around things and squeeze!

Curled up and cozy
Anacondas can slither and slide their way into small holes.

Anaconda

This is the biggest snake in the rain forest! They find it easier to move in the water than on land— and it keeps them cool too!

Cloud Forest

Diego has animal friends in the Cloud Forest—a mountainside forest with clouds hanging right inside it! That makes it a cool, misty place for animals to live, like the tapir and spectacled bear.

Water lovers
Tapirs love to cool off by swimming in lakes or ponds.

Field Journal Update!
Who in the Cloud Forest makes nests in trees?

 Spectacled bears

 Tapirs   Diego

Fur coat
Tapirs have long fur for when it gets chilly!

Baby tapirs have stripes, but lose them when they get older.

Flexible snout for grabbing foliage.

Tapir
The tapir is related to the horse and the rhino. Like both those animals, tapirs eat grass and run really fast!

Spectacled bear

Spectacled bears get their names from the dark patches of fur around their eyes that look like glasses or spectacles!

Fruit finders!

Spectacled bears live in fruit trees because they love to eat fruit!

Climb! ¡Sube! Diego uses a harness to climb a tree...

...But spectacled bears have sharp claws for climbing!

Bird or bear?

Spectacled bears not only live in trees like birds, but build nests for their young too!

Mountain

Diego has scaled some tall peaks to climb to the rescue of animals in trouble. Whether he's helping a hawk migrate down a mountain or helping a chinchilla hop up one, Diego is always ready for a mountain mission with you!

How many animals live in the mountains?

Puma

Pumas live in mountains, forests, grasslands, and even the desert! They're great hunters and excellent climbers who can leap high into the air with their powerful legs!

Excellent hearing helps it find food!

Strong legs for super-leaping!

Lots of other animals are scared of pumas and need to be careful when they're around!

Chinchilla

Chinchillas may be small, but their big ears give them excellent hearing and their big eyes help them see well at night.

Warm, cozy fur for keeping warm on cold mountains.

Time to eat!
What do chinchillas eat? Yummy leaves!

Excellent eyesight for finding food from the sky!

Huge wings from tip to tip are taller than a full-grown man!

Condors don't fly at night, so Diego had to help three babies hurry up Condor Mountain before sunset!

Condor

Condors are the largest flying birds in the world! They have thick feathers around their necks, but none on their head!

39

Ocean

Take a deep dive with Diego to help his undersea animal friends! He may need your help to swim to the rescue or to pilot his Rescue Sub all the way to the ocean floor.

Blowhole for breathing when they come up for air.

Whale shark
This shark has over 3,000 teeth, but it's a gentle giant that only eats small plankton.

Field Journal Update!
Which is the true whale fact?

 Whales are fish.

 Whales are reptiles.

Whales are mammals.

Humpback whale

Humpback whales got that name because when they dive, they bend their backs in a hump!

How many tentacles does an octopus have? *"¡Ocho! Eight!"*

Big tail for splashing and pushing them through water.

Bumpy flippers help them swim gracefully.

The Giant Octopus lives deep in the ocean.

Think ink

A giant octopus can squirt purple ink to help it get away from animals that scare it!

Antarctica

Diego will go to the ends of the Earth for his animal friends—literally! Antarctica may not have as many animals as the rainforest, but if a penguin, seal, or whale needs an icy animal rescue, Diego will be there!

Emperor penguin

Emperor penguins are the biggest of all the penguins. They are great swimmers and can dive really deep.

Chick it out!
Even big emperor penguins start off as small chicks!

Special feathers for swimming and keeping warm!

Whale of a time!

Sperm whale
Sperm whales are the deepest divers in the sea!

Orcas
Orca whales are the largest members of the dolphin family!

Field Journal Update!
Which is the true penguin fact?

- Penguins fly in the sky.
- Penguins swim in the sea.
- Penguins run fast through the desert.

Brrr! Most of Antarctica is covered in ice!

Ice sliding!
To move quickly through the ice, macaroni penguins slide on their bellies!

Macaroni penguin
As they get older, macaroni penguins grow yellow-orange tassels on their heads that look like macaroni!

Macky the macaroni penguin.

Desert

Lots of animals have adapted to life in the desert, where it's hot during the day and cold at night. There's not a lot of water to drink or plants to eat, but these clever creatures know how to survive. And if they do need help, Diego is never very far away!

A speedy bird!
Roadrunners rarely fly. They prefer to run.

Desert iguana

These iguanas live in the desert. They can change their body color to keep from getting too hot or cold.

Long tails for balance!

Long, sharp nails for digging and climbing!

Home sweet hole!
Desert iguanas hibernate in warm holes underground.

Rock climbers
Desert iguanas use their sharp claws to climb.

Grasslands

It's a rescue in the grasslands! Diego has lots of animal friends that live in the tall, cool grass. Some animals use the grass to hide while others just eat it!

Prairie dogs eat grass when they're hungry or thirsty!

Maned wolf

Nice coat! The maned wolf gets its name from the longer hair that grows along its back. It has a mane like a lion or a horse.

Calls out with short, loud barks!

Plenty of pups!
A mommy maned wolf gives birth to a litter of two to six pups at a time.

Long legs to run fast and see over tall grass!

Field Journal Update!

Which of these animals has really long legs?

 Iguana   Prairie dog

 Maned wolf

Africa

Sometimes, Diego travels on special rescue missions, like to the Savanna in Africa. When a mean magician mixed up all the African animals, Diego needed your help on a safari to save them!

Giraffes are one of the few animals born with horns.

Rhino

Charge! When they sense danger, rhinos charge first... and ask questions later.

Like human fingerprints, each giraffe's coat is unique.

Giraffe

The giraffe is the world's tallest land mammal. Its long neck helps it to eat leaves off the tallest trees!

46

Diego, Alicia, and Baby Jaguar pay a visit to African Animal Rescuer, Juma.

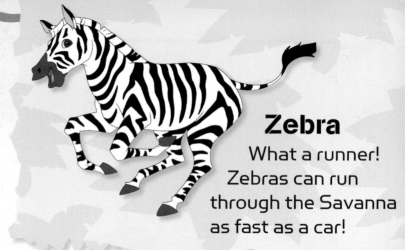

Zebra

What a runner! Zebras can run through the Savanna as fast as a car!

Cool trick! Elephants cool themselves off by flapping their big ears.

Lion

Lions can roar so loudly that they raise a cloud of dust from the ground!

Elephant

Elephants can use their trunks to grab things, spray water, blow dust off themselves, or eat and drink!

Field Journal Update!

Which African animal is the TALLEST land animal?

 Giraffe

 Hippo

 Elephant

London, New York, Munich,
Melbourne, and Delhi

Project Editor Heather Scott
Art Editor Lynne Moulding
Brand Manager Robert Perry
Publishing Manager Simon Beecroft
Category Publisher Alex Allan
Production Nick Seston

First published in the United States in 2008
by DK Publishing
375 Hudson Street, New York, New York 10014

08 09 10 11 12 10 9 8 7 6 5 4 3 2 1
GD102—12/07

DK books are available at special discounts when purchased in bulk for sales promotions,
premiums, fund-raising, or educational use. For details contact: DK Publishing Special
Markets, 375 Hudson Street, New York, New York 10014, SpecialSales@dk.com

A catalog record for this book is available from
the Library of Congress.
ISBN: 978-0-7566-3501-5

Printed and bound in China by Hung Hing

**Discover more at
www. dk.com**

Answers

p13	A parasail	**p43**	Penguins swim in the sea
p20	Sloths move slowly		
p36	Spectacled bears	**p45**	Maned wolf
p40	Whales are fish	**p47**	Giraffe